Ladybird  Readers

The Jungle Book

Series Editor: Sorrel Pitts
Text adapted by Sorrel Pitts
Illustrated by Gavin Scott

LADYBIRD BOOKS

UK | USA | Canada | Ireland | Australia
India | New Zealand | South Africa

Ladybird Books is part of the Penguin Random House group of companies
whose addresses can be found at global.penguinrandomhouse.com.
www.penguin.co.uk   www.puffin.co.uk   www.ladybird.com

Penguin
Random House
UK

First published 2016
001

Copyright © Ladybird Books Ltd, 2016

The moral rights of the author and illustrator have been asserted.

Printed in China

A CIP catalogue record for this book is available from the British Library

ISBN: 978–0–241–25383–0

The Jungle Book

Picture words

jungle

Mother Wolf and
Father Wolf

Baloo the bear

Shere Khan
the tiger

Bagheera the panther

4

monkey

Chil the kite

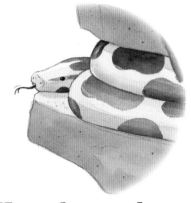

Kaa the python

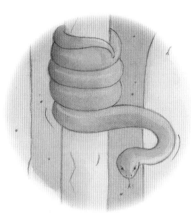

snake

buffalo

Mowgli

One day, Mother Wolf heard a shout in the jungle. Then a little boy ran out of the trees. A big, red tiger ran after him! The tiger's name was Shere Khan.

"We must help that little boy,"
Mother Wolf told Father Wolf.
"He can stay with us. Let's call
him Mowgli."

Shere Khan was angry. He wanted
to eat the little boy.

"I'm coming back for him," he said.

"You must learn to make jungle calls, Mowgli," said Baloo the bear. He made some loud noises. "Then you can talk to the animals."

Bagheera the panther heard about Mowgli and he came to say hello.

Mowgli wanted to play with the monkeys.

But Baloo and Bagheera said, "You mustn't play with the monkeys. They are very bad. You are not safe with monkeys."

The next day, the bear and the panther were very tired. They slept all afternoon. Two monkeys came and they took Mowgli to their tree. Mowgli was afraid!

Mowgli saw Chil the kite.
He made a jungle call and Chil
flew down.

"Find Baloo and Bagheera,"
Mowgli said. "Tell them to help me!"

Chil quickly found Baloo and Bagheera. "The monkeys have got Mowgli!" he said.

"Ask Kaa the python to help us," Bagheera said. "The monkeys don't like him and they are afraid of him."

19

The monkeys put Mowgli in a snake house. But Mowgli made a jungle call and the snakes did not come near him.

Then, Mowgli saw Bagheera the panther! The monkeys jumped on Bagheera and bit him.

"Go in the water!" Mowgli called.

When Baloo came to help, the monkeys jumped on him, too!

Then, the monkeys saw Kaa the python and they ran away!

Soon, Mowgli was safe with Baloo and Bagheera again.

Mowgli lived with the wolves in the jungle. But one day, Bagheera the panther said, "The wolves do not want a little boy with them. They want a strong, young wolf. You are not strong or fast because you are not a wolf."

"You are not safe here, Mowgli," said Bagheera. "You must go to the village and live with people."

"But I am as strong as a wolf!" Mowgli said. "I must kill Shere Khan and show his body to the wolves."

Mowgli went to the village and all the people came out to see him. "That is my son!" said a woman called Messua. And Mowgli went to live with her.

33

In the village, Mowgli worked with the buffaloes. He took them to find food and water.

One day, two wolves came to see Mowgli. One of the wolves was called Gray Brother.

"Shere Khan came back. He wants to eat you," said Gray Brother.

"Take the buffaloes with you," said Mowgli. "They can help me."

When the tiger came, Mowgli called the buffaloes.

They ran to Shere Khan and killed him!

Mowgli took the tiger's body to the village.

The village people said, "We want that tiger's body."

"It's mine!" said Mowgli. The people were very angry.

"You have got to go," Messua said. "You are not safe here now."

Mowgli went back to the jungle.

The wolves saw Shere Khan's body, "You can live with us!" they said. "You are as strong as a wolf."

But Mowgli said, "No, you did not want me to live with you before."

"I'm sorry," said Gray Brother.
"Please live with me now."

Mowgli went to live with Gray
Brother in the jungle.

And Baloo and Bagheera were
happy because Mowgli was safe.

Activities

The key below describes the skills practiced in each activity.

Spelling and writing

Reading

Speaking

? Critical thinking

Preparation for the Cambridge Young Learners Exams

1 **Look and read. Choose the correct words and write them on the lines.** 📖 ✏️ ✩

jungle   tiger   wolf   panther

1 This is the place where monkeys and snakes live.

........jungle........

2 This is the animal who gave Mowgli his name.

Mother wolf

3 This is the animal who came to say hello to Mowgli.

Bageera

4 This is the animal who wanted to eat Mowgli.

Shere khan

2 **Look and read. Choose the correct words and write them on the lines.** 📖 ✏️ ✲

jungle

Mowgli

tiger

Mother Wolf

1 One day, Mother Wolf heard a shout in the ___jungle___ .

2 A big, red ___tiger___ ran after a little boy.

3 "We must help that little boy," said ___Mother wolf___.

4 "He can stay with us. Let's call him ___Mowgli___ ."

3 **Work with a friend.**
Talk about the two pictures.
How are they different? 💬

a

One day, Mother Wolf heard a shout in the jungle. Then a little boy ran out of the trees. A big, red tiger ran after him! The tiger's name was Shere Khan.

b

"We must help that little boy," Mother Wolf told Father Wolf. "He can stay with us. Let's call him Mowgli."

Shere Khan was angry. He wanted to eat the little boy.

"I'm coming back for him," he said.

Example:

In picture a, we can see Mother Wolf.

In picture b, we can see Mother Wolf and Father Wolf.

4 **Find the words.**

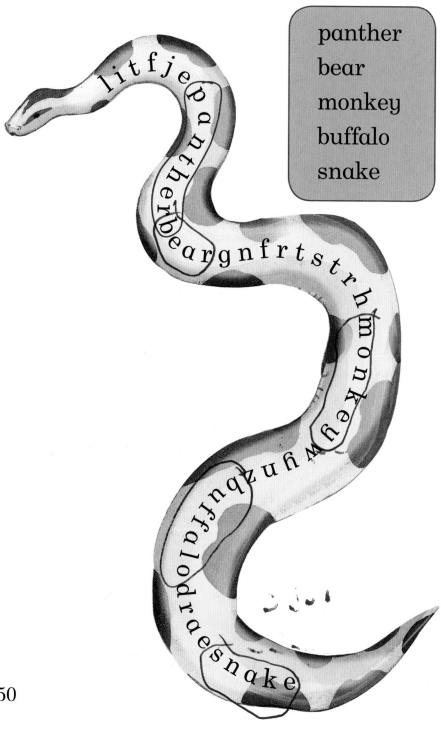

panther
bear
monkey
buffalo
snake

50

5 **Look and read. Choose the correct words and write them on the lines.** 📖 ✏️ ⭐

> flew   made   play   safe   slept

1 "You mustn't _play_ with the

monkeys," said Baloo and Bagheera.

2 "You aren't _safe_ with

monkeys," they said.

3 When the bear and the panther

slept, two monkeys came

and took Mowgli.

4 When Mowgli saw Chil the kite, he

made a jungle call.

5 Chil _flew_ down to Mowgli.

6 **Work with a friend.**
Talk about the two pictures.
How are they different? 💬

When Baloo came to help, the monkeys jumped on him, too!

Then, the monkeys saw Kaa the python and they ran away!

Soon, Mowgli was safe with Baloo and Bagheera again.

Example:

In picture a, Mowgli is in the snake house.

In picture b, Mowgli is with Baloo.

7 Circle the correct word.

Mowgli lived with the wolves in the jungle. But one day, Bagheera the panther said, "The wolves do not want a little boy with them. They want a strong, young wolf. You are not strong or fast because you are not a wolf."

1 When **Kaa** / **Baloo** came to help, the monkeys jumped on him, too!

2 When the monkeys saw Kaa the **kite** / **python**, they ran away!

3 Soon, Mowgli was **safe** / **afraid** with Baloo and Bagheera again.

4 One day, Bagheera said, "The wolves do not want a little **wolf** / **boy** with them."

5 Bagheera said to Mowgli, "You are not strong or fast **because** / **when** you are not a wolf."

8 Read the questions. Write answers using words in the box. ✏️ 📖

> people village
>
> show to wolves Shere Khan

1 Where did Bagheera tell Mowgli he must go?

He must go to the village.

2 Who did Bagheera want Mowgli to live with?

people

3 Who did Mowgli want to kill?

Shere Khan

4 What did Mowgli want to do with the tiger's body?

Show it to the village people

9 Look at the pictures. One picture is different. How is it different? Tell your teacher.

In picture a,
Shere Khan is dead.

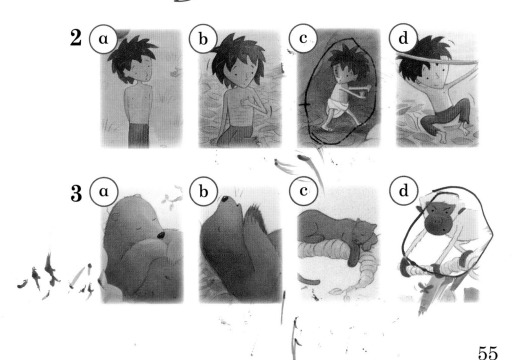

10 **Read the text and circle the best answer.** 📖 ⬡

1 Bagheera said, "You are not .... a wolf."

   a (as strong as)

   b as strong

2 The jungle wasn't .... the village for Mowgli.

   a safer

   b (as safe as)

3 Messua said, "You have got to go. You .... here now."

   a (are safe)

   b are not safe

4 Mowgli went back to the jungle. The wolves said to Mowgli, "You are .... a wolf."

   a stronger than

   b (as strong as)

11 Ask and answer the questions with a friend. 💬 ❓

1 *Who did Mowgli go to live with?*

He went to live with Gray Brother.

2 Was Gray Brother sorry about the past?

3 Who did Mowgli see again when he went back to the jungle?

4 Was Mowgli happier in the village or in the jungle, do you think?

Circle the correct picture.

1 What did Mowgli do in the snake house to make him safe?

a   b

2 What did the monkeys do to Bagheera?

a   b

3 Which animal frightened
the monkeys?

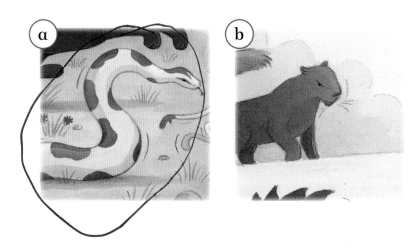

a   b

4 Which animal opened the
snake house and took Mowgli?

a   b

13 Ask and answer questions about the picture with a friend. 🗨

Mowgli took the tiger's body to the village.

The village people said, "We want that tiger's body."

"It's mine!" said Mowgli. The people were very angry.

"You have got to go," Messua said. "You are not safe here now."

40   41

Example:

> Who is Mowgli talking to?

> He's talking to Messua, his mother.

14 **Read the text and choose the best answer.**

1 Did Mowgli use the jungle calls with the snakes?

a Yes, he did.　　**b** Yes, he could.

2 How did Kaa the python help Mowgli?

a He bit Bagheera and Baloo.

b He frightened the monkeys.

3 Why did Gray Brother go to see Mowgli?

a He wanted to tell him about Shere Khan.

b He wanted to tell him about Mother Wolf.

4 Why didn't Mowgli stay with Messua?

a The village people were angry with Mowgli.

b She was angry with Mowgli.

15 **Ask and answer the questions with a friend.** ○

1

Who is your favorite animal in the story? Why?

My favorite animal is a bear because it is big.

2 Would you like to live in the jungle with animals? Why? No so M eare Dangerous

3 Would you like to have any of these animals in your house? Why?

Snake for a pet

4 Why were the monkeys not Mowgli's friends? they captured him

5 Are you frightened of any of the animals in the story? Why? No 'cause i like them all esspecily ssssnakess

16 **Write who or where.**

1 That is the house ___where___ the snakes live.

2 Those are the monkeys ___who___ bit Bagheera.

3 That water is the place ___where___ Bagheera was safe.

4 Kaa is the one ___who___ frightened the monkeys.

5 The jungle is the place ___where___ the story started and ended.

Level 3

Sharks

978-0-241-25382-3

The Jungle Book

978-0-241-25383-0

The Red Knight

978-0-241-25384-7

The Elves and the Shoemaker

978-0-241-25385-4

Now you're ready for Level 4!

Notes
CEFR levels are based on guidelines set out in the Council of Europe's European Framework. Cambridge Young Learners English (YLE) Exams give a reliable indication of a child's progression in learning English.